Disney's
Winnie the Pooh
Home Sweet Home

It's nice to Visit places

And play with friends you know.

But I can't wait

To hurry home

'Cause someone loves me so.

One very sunny Sunday, Roo went to Rabbit's house. They worked in the garden all day long and had a wonderful time picking carrots, lettuce, and tomatoes.

But when it was time to leave, Roo didn't want to go home. "Why, Roo," said Rabbit, "Kanga is waiting for you. You don't want to be late for supper, do you?"

Roo didn't care. "There's nothing to do at my house," he complained. "I don't have a big garden like yours!"

Rabbit listened as he put some vegetables in a basket for Roo to take with him.

"It's getting late, and I'm afraid that Kanga will worry. Let's go, Roo," Rabbit insisted.

So Roo took Rabbit's hand, and they left for home.

When they got to Roo's house, Kanga was waiting for them.
    "Oh, Roo," she said, hugging him, "I missed you. I'm so glad
you're home."
    Roo didn't answer. He just sighed a very big sigh.

The next day was Monday. Kanga thought it would be nice to take Roo over to Owl's house.

Roo spent the whole day listening to Owl tell the most amazing stories.

Soon it was time to leave, but Roo didn't want to go home.

"Tut-tut-tut, young fellow," Owl insisted. "It's important to listen to your mama."

A reluctant Roo hopped into Kanga's pouch and left.

On Tuesday, Roo went to Pooh's house, where he played a little game of musical chairs with Pooh, Piglet, and Tigger.

After supper, Kanga appeared at Pooh's door. "Come, Roo," she called. "Time to go home."

"Five more minutes, Mama," Roo called, going back to play. Kanga spoke up again.

"I'm having fun," Roo sighed. "I don't want to go home."

When Kanga gently insisted, Roo said goodbye to his friends.

"What's wrong?" Kanga asked Roo on their way home.

"I like playing at my friends' homes more than I do at my home," he explained.

"Well," said Kanga, "let's see what we can do about that."

On Wednesday, Kanga invited Roo's friends over for the day. She wanted Roo to see that he could have a good time playing at his house, too.

First Roo asked if they could bake cookies.

"What a good idea, Roo," Kanga said, getting out the ingredients. Soon the cookies were ready.

"These are the best cookies I've ever tasted," Piglet said.

Next, they had a wonderful time playing with Roo's toys.
They took piles of blocks and stacked them up to the ceiling!
Pooh's stack kept falling over. "Oh, bother," he sighed.
"I'm not very good with blocks."

"Hoo-hoo-hoo," laughed Tigger, making shorter stacks. "Let's see who can bounce over these blocks!"

Of course, it was Tigger, because everyone knows bouncing is what tiggers do best.

Next they painted lovely pictures.

"Mine's a rainbow," Piglet said, admiring his work.

"Mine's a honey pot overflowing with scrumdelicious hunny," Pooh announced, licking his lips.

When they were finished, Kanga took Roo's paintbox and lined up all his friends.

Then she painted a star on Roo's cheek, a butterfly on Pooh, a flower on Tigger, a heart on Piglet, and a balloon on Eeyore.

"Gee, Little Buddy," said Tigger, looking in Roo's mirror. "I've never looked better!"

"Thanks, Mama," Roo cried. "You're the best!"

Kanga smiled happily. Her plan was working.

After that, Roo and his friends went outside to play a quick game of hide-and-seek.

"Hoo-hoo-hoo!" Tigger cried. "Ready or not, here I come!"

When they were thirsty, Piglet and Roo made fresh lemonade.
"What should we do now?" asked Roo.
"Kanga, would you read us a story?" Pooh suggested.

"Of course," Kanga said.

When it was time to go, Pooh and his friends didn't want to leave. They were having too much fun.

"Do we really have to go?" Eeyore asked.

Kanga had an idea. "Would you like to stay and camp out under the stars?" she asked.

"Can we really, Mama?" Roo asked, overjoyed.

"Of course you may," Kanga replied.

What a wonderful day it had been! And from that day on, Roo knew that he had the very best home of all.

A LESSON A DAY
POOH'S WAY

There's no place like home

with Kanga!